Havana Journal

by Eduardo Machado

A SAMUEL FRENCH ACTING EDITION

MUSIC USE NOTE

Licensees are solely responsible for obtaining formal written permission from copyright owners to use copyrighted music in the performance of this play and are strongly cautioned to do so. If no such permission is obtained by the licensee, then the licensee must use only original music that the licensee owns and controls. Licensees are solely responsible and liable for all music clearances and shall indemnify the copyright owners of the play and their licensing agent, Samuel French, Inc., against any costs, expenses, losses and liabilities arising from the use of music by licensees.

IMPORTANT BILLING AND CREDIT
REQUIREMENTS

All producers of *HAVANA JOURNAL must* give credit to the Author of the Play in all programs distributed in connection with performances of the Play, and in all instances in which the title of the Play appears for the purposes of advertising, publicizing or otherwise exploiting the Play and/or a production. The name of the Author *must* appear on a separate line on which no other name appears, immediately following the title and *must* appear in size of type not less than fifty percent of the size of the title type.

HAVANA JOURNAL was first produced by the Theater for the New City (Crystal Field, Executive Director) and INTAR Theatre (Eduardo Machado, Artistic Director) in New York City on March 26, 2010. The performance was directed by Stefanie Sertich, with scenic and lighting design by Maruti Evans, costumes by Michael Bevins, sound by Elizabeth Rhodes, and original music by Michael Moricz. The production stage manager was Michael Alifanz. The cast was as follows:

RUTH . . . . Crystal Field

IVAN . . . . .David Skeist

REYNALDO . . . . Juan Javier Cardenas

TOM . . . . .Liam Torres

CHARACTERS

RUTH - a woman in her early seventies
IVAN - a young Russian man
REYNALDO - a Cuban man in his forties
TOM - an American man in his fifties

SETTING

New York City and Havana, Cuba

TIME

2004

For Megan Smith

Scene One

(A stage – only furniture and lights.)

(All the characters are onstage. They walk in to play their scenes. When they are not on in a scene, they wear earphones and are listening to something in the shadows.)

(Slide: Columbia University, New York, May, 2004.)

(An office. Late at night. A desk, a couple of chairs, a filing cabinet. A couple of lamps. A few plants. A worn-out oriental rug. Stacks of folders and manuscripts. **RUTH**, *a woman in her early seventies, locks the door to her office. She glances at one of the folders.)*

RUTH. Not risking anything in that short story. What are your secret longings? You, vain, rich, entitled, twenty-five year-old white male...But then again, Ruth, you are the one that sold yourself out by teaching here. Ivy League. Ivy League? Sometimes I wish I could hang myself from the fucking ivy!

*(***RUTH*** looks at another folder.)*

Oh, honey. Girl? You are in grad school for God's sake. Be a woman! Why do you still want to be Daddy's good little girl. Don't you know that writers are evil? Fucking Republicans! God! You teach the children of Republicans and well meaning pseudo liberals. Because a real radical would never allow their child to get a "Masters" in fiction writing. Read. Get it over with. Crap! Just give me one student with a revolutionary idea. Please! They all want to win the Pulitzer. That's the only reason they come here. Or worse, write novels so they can get a movie deal. Maybe when they start the draft again they will finally have to face the truth. When they are in the fucking army.

7

(We hear a door open and close.)

RUTH. *(cont.)* Sandor, is that you?

(She opens the door. She looks out into the hallway.)

No. You are most likely fucking your young Czechoslovakian story editor. Why am I talking to myself? Because your students' literary aspirations are enough to drive anyone insane.

(She opens a drawer, takes a fifth of vodka. Opens it. Takes a sip.)

Come on! Get over it! Grade them. Sandor, why am I obsessed with Sandor? Why don't my students write about obsession? They're too afraid to be obsessed. No wonder we have George W. as a president. He is as inarticulate as they are. Getting bitter. Time for secret thoughts. Why am I in love with a sixty-something-year-old, once famous Czechoslovakian short story writer? We are back to that? Time for the secret tapes. Document everything, every little detail of your struggle. Question everything, and then you have material. Can't you understand that? Students? Idiots! Cowards!

(She throws a few folders to the floor.)

All my students in the end are cowards. At first...the first year you hope that one will be brave. One will change the form. One will connect with the volcano inside of them. But never, not once in now...what? Thirty years of teaching. In the beginning there were some great ones, but Capitalism got the best of them... the ones that could moved to L.A. and got rich...What a disappointment. Go to the tapes, forget.

*(**RUTH** gets a key from a bottom drawer and unlocks her filing cabinet. She opens a drawer filled with tapes.)*

My material. My longings, my life. My secrets. Nixon had secret tapes, so do I. If Ben ever found them, it would have killed him. It's a good thing he's dead... Poor Ben, poor husband...I met you when I was twenty and you were forty at a socialist study group. You knew your Marx backwards and forwards, and you swept me off my feet. Too bad we never had children, Ben. How smart would they have been?

(She looks at the tape recorder.)

RUTH. *(cont.)* Still an hour's worth of tape left, good.

(She pushes "record.")

Hello, Ruth. I can't write a word lately...well, for a year...so I have started talking...I am talking to you now as before, when you are seventy-two. It's late May, Columbia University, and the Republicans have been here again for four years...I am still trying to read the first years' work from last semester...and it is still tedious. They will be back in September. Still blank pages. And I am still aching for Sandor...who will be leaving soon to spend the summer in the south of France...with one or two of his mistresses. And Ben has been dead now for such a long time.

(The sound of a door opening and closing.)

And I just heard a door open and close and my heart stopped because I thought it would be Sandor, my secret obsession, compulsion....and we are as I speak continuing to destroy Iraq...humiliating them, raping them...And I know I should care. I should speak out. Write an article for "The Nation"...But all I can think about is that my knees are still bruised from when Sandor fucked me right here on my oriental rug. And I am still wondering if he really came or faked it... Why doesn't he come all the time?...'Cause he saves his sperm for all the young girls in his harem...but I do respect him...I mean he stood up for the workers... he did live under State control, Marxism, Leninism, Stalinism...And yet he still believes in fairness...in Marx's fundamental teachings...he knows this country is going to the dogs...he does think outside the box, and for that I do love him...I do want him, and the only times I...speak out...are when he is fucking me on all fours on that oriental rug...I'm so afraid someone is going to tell me to be quiet. I am so afraid they're going to silence me. That they are going to take my memory away. That's what these Republicans want, to take our memories away...Example: always give an example...Our civil rights, our reproductive rights, our freedom to speak out...God. I hate you, Sandor...no, I don't...If you're listening to this...I don't hate you. Sometimes I wish you secretly listened to my tapes... Time for a drink...Too many true confessions.

(She goes to get a drink. The door opens.)

RUTH. Sandor? You've come.

IVAN. You are here. Sorry.

(A young Russian man is standing there. He is in a custodian's uniform.)

IVAN. I clean your offices, yours and Sandor's.

RUTH. Well. I'm still working.

IVAN. Any trash?

RUTH. Sure, clean it.

IVAN. Taping a speech?

RUTH. A lecture.

IVAN. Professor, of course.

RUTH. Yes. I am looking for the truth.

IVAN. Are you?

RUTH. Yes!

IVAN. The truth has many sides.

RUTH. Nevermind, don't clean my office.

IVAN. Fine.

RUTH. Didn't mean to be mean. I'm busy.

IVAN. Sure.

RUTH. I'm going on a trip.

IVAN. Vacation?

RUTH. Not really.

IVAN. Oh.

RUTH. Research.

IVAN. Of course, you are a professor.

RUTH. Yes, I am.

IVAN. Good. I'm Ivan.

RUTH. Nice to meet you, Ivan, I'm Ruth.

IVAN. I know.

RUTH. How do you know?

IVAN. Your name on door.

RUTH. Right.

IVAN. I will clean tomorrow.

RUTH. Good.

IVAN. Yes, well...

RUTH. Fine, tomorrow.

IVAN. Fine.

RUTH. Good night.

IVAN. Yes, good night.

(He goes. She talks into the recorder.)

RUTH. I am going to Cuba soon, maybe Cuba will pose the right kind of questions. I know it's not utopia, I know it's state controlled...Capitalism...Am I being bugged? Will they stop my trip to Cuba? Will you stop my trip to Cuba? George, are you listening to me? Or is your mother, Barbara? Or maybe it's your dad, the other George?

(Blackout.)

(In the shadows the men sing.)

MEN.

TAKE A CUP OF HOLY WATER
THEN PERFUME THE SWEET WARM WATER.
FILL YOUR SOUL TO OVERFLOWING
FOR OUR JOURNEY WITH YEMAYA.
YEMAYA, YEMAYA.

TAKE HER NECKLACE.
FEEL HER POWER.

MEN. *(cont.)*
> LET IT BATHE IN THE MILK FROM A COCONUT
> WASH THE NECKLACE IN THE OCEAN
> FEEL THAT OCEAN FLOW INSIDE YOU
> SWEET YEMAYA
> YEMAYA, YEMAYA.
>
> TASTE THE SALT WITHIN YOUR TEARS
> NEVER SEEK TO HIDE THEM
> TELL HER ALL YOUR DREAMS AND FEARS
> AND THE QUEEN WILL GUIDE THEM
> SWEET YEMAYA
> SWEET YEMAYA
> SWEET YEMAYA
>
> WE HAVE PLACED
> OUR CUP OF WATER,
> WE HAVE FILLED A JAR WITH HONEY.
> AND WE DRINK THE CANE'S SWEET NECTAR
> AND YOUR BOWL IS FILLED WITH SEA.
> COME AND JOIN OUR SACRED PARTY.
> FILL OUR SOULS TO OVERFLOWING
> DO NOT HIDE
> BE OUR GUIDE
> HELP US FIND YOUR TRUEST MEANING.
> SWEET YEMAYA
> SWEET YEMAYA
> SWEET YEMAYA
> SWEET YEMAYA

IVAN. Sweet Yemaya...
> Sweet Yemaya...

Scene Two

(A slide reads: June, 2004. El Malecon. Havana, Cuba.)

*(**REYNALDO**, a Cuban man in his forties, is sitting with* **RUTH.** *They are listening to a CD on Ruth's Discman. They each have one earplug in their ears.)*

RUTH. Beautiful.

REYNALDO. Strong violin, huh?

RUTH. Yes.

REYNALDO. And it is an all-woman band.

RUTH. I know. Janet told me. Women playing classical music...

REYNALDO. Very proud.

RUTH. Are you playing?

REYNALDO. No, I'm the conductor, arranger, everything.

RUTH. A man?

REYNALDO. Yes.

RUTH. Leading women?

REYNALDO. Yes.

RUTH. Great. Nothing ever changes.

REYNALDO. Were you being sarcastic?

RUTH. Yes, of course I was.

REYNALDO. Enough for now.

>   (**REYNALDO** *turns off the Walkman. They take the earplugs out of their ears.*)

RUTH. I want to hear more.

REYNALDO. Later.

RUTH. It's wonderful.

REYNALDO. Classical.

RUTH. Yes.

REYNALDO. A historian said that this is the most important thing to happen in Cuban culture for the last hundred years.

RUTH. Your group?

REYNALDO. My group, yes, my knowledge as a conductor. My art.

RUTH. It is beautiful.

REYNALDO. Thank you. But also important.

RUTH. Yes. I can hear it.

REYNALDO. It proves that women can play as good as men.

RUTH. With you conducting them?

REYNALDO. Of course.

RUTH. I guess "machismo" never goes away.

REYNALDO. Why should it?

RUTH. Because it should!

REYNALDO. I thought you were a Marxist?

RUTH. Not a Fidelista.

REYNALDO. Don't say that.

RUTH. I'm an American, I can say whatever I want.

REYNALDO. You are here illegally.

RUTH. So what!

REYNALDO. Were you blacklisted?

RUTH. No. My late husband was.

REYNALDO. Then you should know about being quiet.

RUTH. I would never have named names.

REYNALDO. You never know.

RUTH. I know.

REYNALDO. So certain?

RUTH. Yes. Absolutely.

REYNALDO. When people think Cuban music, they think...

RUTH. Buena Vista Social Club?

REYNALDO. What else?

RUTH. I don't know, Mambo, Cha-cha-chá...Drums...

REYNALDO. Please. That's popular, this is classical.

RUTH. Yes. Janet told me how dedicated she is to you, and
she was so happy that I was taking a chance to come
here...

REYNALDO. Even though George W. Bush has made it all so
much more illegal. A criminal act.

RUTH. Yes.

REYNALDO. Five hundred page documents about regime
change in Cuba.

RUTH. It's just election year politics.

REYNALDO. Don't be so sure.

RUTH. What?

REYNALDO. He wants to rule the world.

RUTH. I know that, believe me, I know that...I'm not some...

REYNALDO. What?

RUTH. Average American.

REYNALDO. Are you the kind that thinks they didn't know about the plans to destroy the towers?

RUTH. Well. Now we know they knew. I don't doubt anything from the son of a bitch! From any of them, the Democrats aren't much better either. They started the Embargo. Kennedy.

REYNALDO. Here in Cuba, as soon as the planes crashed we knew it was some kind of CIA plot.

RUTH. You think a CIA plot?

REYNALDO. Wait and see.

RUTH. Well, I don't know. I frankly think the CIA was kept out of it. I think this is some kind of deal between the Royal Saudi family and the Bushes. I mean, I think the CIA was out of it.

REYNALDO. Remember the Maine.

RUTH. What?

REYNALDO. A huge boat at the turn of the century that your government blew up. Right there in the Harbor.

RUTH. Right. So they would have a reason to get into the Spanish American War. So they could colonize you. Teddy Roosevelt, you mean?

REYNALDO. Teddy Roosevelt was no hero.

RUTH. He was a monster. He started Manifest Destiny and all of that bullshit. A total monster.

REYNALDO. Yes, he was.

RUTH. He blew up an American boat?

REYNALDO. Yes.

RUTH. Here on the Bay?

REYNALDO. Yes, he did.

RUTH. I didn't know that.

REYNALDO. Full of American sailors. They said the Spaniards blew it up. The Spaniards denied it...but it was too late, the "Rough Riders" were already attacking, invading.

RUTH. Then you were under U.S. control 'til the Revolution. In one way or another. Right? Then you had a Revolution and you have lived without us for over four decades. You have managed to continue without us. That's why I'm here.

REYNALDO. Janet said you were smart. That I would like you. I love Janet.

RUTH. So do I.

REYNALDO. I respect her. She respects you. So here we are.

RUTH. Well, she trusted me with all this money.

REYNALDO. You counted it?

RUTH. No, of course not. But I mean...it's a heavy envelope. You'll see.

(**RUTH** *takes out the envelope.*)

RUTH. Here.

REYNALDO. Thank you.

RUTH. Sure.

REYNALDO. You know what this means.

RUTH. Not really.

REYNALDO. We can afford a violin, pantyhose for my all women orchestra. Recording equipment. We mixed all this, the whole CD, in my garage.

RUTH. It's wonderful. I want to listen to more of it.

REYNALDO. Art is a wonderful thing.

RUTH. Yes, it is.

REYNALDO. Why does your President want to make everything so much harder?

RUTH. To win Florida. Fucking bastard.

REYNALDO. I won't be able to see my brother.

RUTH. What?

REYNALDO. He already came this year. And he is too old to come illegally. He's my half-brother from my father's first marriage. We grew up apart. Like so many people here. But while Clinton was President and things loosened, I toured Ohio, Atlanta, Santa Fe, Berkeley. He came to my concerts. We grew close. The new law, set up by your President so they can win Florida, only allows a brother to visit his brother once every three years. Under Clinton, it was every year. Things were opening up. When my orchestra toured the Midwest, we made friends with the Yankees. We saw a future.

RUTH. Your brother, he was proud?

REYNALDO. Yes. I think so.

RUTH. It felt good?

REYNALDO. To connect again.

RUTH. Yes.

REYNALDO. My brother was helping me financially and spiritually, and now for the Florida vote this bastard has shut the door again.

RUTH. He's a hypocrite.

REYNALDO. They want to rule us.

RUTH. They want to rule everyone. Believe me.

REYNALDO. I believe you.

RUTH. Why do we want so much?

REYNALDO. What?

RUTH. We want to control everybody else. For what? Oil?

REYNALDO. Oil, money, power, you know.

(**REYNALDO** *laughs.*)

RUTH. We want it more than happiness. More than health care, more than our civil rights. More than peace of mind, more than the future.

REYNALDO. What's wrong with your country?

RUTH. A lot of scared people.

REYNALDO. Scared people everywhere.

RUTH. Here, too?

REYNALDO. Sure, this is not paradise.

RUTH. Right.

REYNALDO. He's not an angel.

RUTH. Who?

REYNALDO. The bearded one.

> *(He indicates a beard with his hands.)*

RUTH. What?

REYNALDO. The horse.

RUTH. Who?

REYNALDO. Fidel!

RUTH. Oh. Right, slang...

REYNALDO. We never refer to his real name when we are... complaining, gossiping about things...him....The bearded one....

> *(He indicates a beard with his hands.)*

RUTH. Oh.

REYNALDO. You see?

RUTH. In America, all of politics have become gossip.

REYNALDO. I know.

RUTH. Idiots on television.

REYNALDO. You know, sometimes I think that no news is better than stupid news.

RUTH. I think you're right.

REYNALDO. I mean, when you judge life for what it is. Not what they tell you. No propaganda. Just the way you are living it. What actually affects you. Not what they tell you is affecting you...

RUTH. Explain this to me.

REYNALDO. Making up your own mind, that's a much better way to live.

RUTH. Right. I do that.

REYNALDO. Within minutes of its release...that paper by Colin Powell, about how they wanted regime change here...everybody knew. How dare they say that! If we want regime change, we will do it. How dare they dictate?

RUTH. They're ruthless.

REYNALDO. Yes, they are.

RUTH. Within minutes you said?

REYNALDO. Within minutes, everyone in Cuba knew about it. The news passed from person to person. That they were cutting the amount of money our relatives could send us...

RUTH. I know.

REYNALDO. That's going to ruin a lot of families' lives.

RUTH. I know. I'm sorry.

REYNALDO. But the worst is that our families cannot visit us, only once every three years. Why? It's none of their business. My brother is a retired teacher, I am an artist. My music gives his life meaning. So he sends me money. Janet believes in me, so she contributes. What's wrong with that? And art has to be subsidized. Don't they know that in your country?

RUTH. No.

REYNALDO. Why?

RUTH. They don't care about art.

REYNALDO. How about families?

RUTH. They pretend to care about families.

REYNALDO. True.

RUTH. I mean, we don't even have a health care system.

REYNALDO. We do.

RUTH. I know. Very impressive.

REYNALDO. I would love to have you to my house for dinner. A drink.

RUTH. You don't have to.

REYNALDO. But I want to.

RUTH. Really. I would like to, I mean, continue this dialectical conversation.

REYNALDO. Dialectical? No.

RUTH. No?

REYNALDO. That was not what I was doing.

RUTH. I like it that you are so smart. I feel very alienated in my country. Sometimes I think I am paranoid.

REYNALDO. We like making friends.

RUTH. I'm not rich!

REYNALDO. It's not about the money. I love Janet. I would still love her if she had never sent this envelope. You believe me?

RUTH. I want to. I mean, I know you need the dollar...

REYNALDO. But that is not...how do you Americans say it? The bottom line.

RUTH. What?

REYNALDO. The dollar is not the bottom line.

RUTH. You believe in community, I can tell.

REYNALDO. Well, in my life the bottom line is humanity and art.

RUTH. Humanity and art. What a wonderful thought.

REYNALDO. How we live with each other.

RUTH. That's why I've come.

REYNALDO. Thank you for the envelope. You have my number, right?

RUTH. Yes.

REYNALDO. Good, please call me. We will make you dinner tomorrow, I will invite some interesting people. I will email Janet today and tell her how you got the envelope to me. And that you are happy. Yes? No?

RUTH. I am.

REYNALDO. Which one?

RUTH. Happy.

REYNALDO. Good.

RUTH. Thanks. I like you a lot.

REYNALDO. I know you do. And I want to know you.

RUTH. What a nice thing to say.

REYNALDO. It's the truth. Dinner tomorrow?

RUTH. Tomorrow. Yes. Of course.

REYNALDO. Fine. You are not a vegetarian, are you?

RUTH. No, me? God, no!

REYNALDO. Good. Well. Until tomorrow, my new friend.

> (**REYNALDO** *embraces* **RUTH.**)

RUTH. Yes. There's ten thousand dollars in there.

REYNALDO. You counted it?

RUTH. Yes, I did.

REYNALDO. Well. You had to know what you were giving me.

RUTH. Yes, I did.

REYNALDO. You are an American after all.

RUTH. But I've come to change. I know I have to change. See something different. So I can get my voice back.

REYNALDO. Your voice?

RUTH. My country has taken it away from me. But here I feel so free. I'll get myself back. I know. I know I will!

REYNALDO. You will.

> (**REYNALDO** *starts to walk away.*)

RUTH. Wait, your CD!

REYNALDO. No, it's for you.

RUTH. I couldn't.

REYNALDO. To enjoy.

RUTH. Enjoy?

REYNALDO. Classical music from the golden age of Cuban music. The eighteen hundreds. We go way back. Further than you.

RUTH. Thank you.

REYNALDO. If he wins again.

RUTH. George W.?

REYNALDO. Mark my words, he will try to destroy us.

RUTH. All this history?

REYNALDO. All of it. History will not absolve him. History is his enemy, it will hold him accountable. It will show how guilty he really is.

RUTH. He cannot win. I won't let him win!

REYNALDO. I asked my Santera if he was going to win or not.

RUTH. Santera?

REYNALDO. My spiritual guide.

RUTH. But religion is the opium of the masses.

REYNALDO. It's not a religion. It's African slaves coming back from the dead. To show us the way.

RUTH. How?

REYNALDO. They can see the future, who you should be in love with, how to get someone to be in love with you... things of the heart, an examination of the soul.

RUTH. I want to see that. I want to experience it. How wonderful.

REYNALDO. African slaves coming to guide us, that is revolution.

RUTH. Yes it is. You are right. You'll take me to see it?

REYNALDO. Only if you want to believe. It's not a tourist attraction.

RUTH. Of course I want to believe.

REYNALDO. You want to find your soul?

RUTH. I want to let it out.

REYNALDO. I can see that.

RUTH. I come from a soulless country.

REYNALDO. Capitalism is without a soul.

RUTH. Yes, it is.

REYNALDO. You are smart.

RUTH. I want to believe. I want to speak up. I want the Revolution to happen again.

REYNALDO. In you?

RUTH. Yes. In me.

REYNALDO. Good. Then you've come to the right country.

RUTH. I feel I have.

REYNALDO. You have, believe me. We wear our souls on our foreheads.

RUTH. That's why you are all so beautiful.

REYNALDO. Thank you.

RUTH. I work at Columbia University, in New York, a cold dry place. If I can find my soul…Then I will make everybody else follow me! Follow me! You see?

REYNALDO. Dinner at around nine p.m.

RUTH. Sure.

REYNALDO. I'll try to find a pork leg.

RUTH. Delicious.

(**REYNALDO** *goes.*)

RUTH. His CD.

(She takes out her tape recorder.)

RUTH. They care about community. They are so warm, they are so fucking smart. They are struggling…still…They are alive, the sea crashing against the walls. Listen to the CD. The breeze from the gulf is intoxicating, and most of all they believe that Capitalism is evil. Listen to the music, Ruth.

(She listens to the CD, we also hear it.)

RUTH. The strings are strong. And women are playing? They call out to you, the violins, with power, sensuality, and need. And women are playing them. Strong, full, real. With a past.

Scene Three

(Slide: El Malecon. Later that day.)

(**REYNALDO** *is greeting* **TOM,** *an American in his fif-ties.* **TOM** *is dressed in Bermuda shorts and a Hawaiian shirt. He takes a picture of* **REYNALDO.***)*

REYNALDO. Is that really necessary?

TOM. Yes, it is.

REYNALDO. Why?

TOM. I'm a tourist. I have to bring pictures to show my buddies back home.

REYNALDO. Of me?

TOM. Of everything I see.

REYNALDO. Of course, right.

TOM. Smile.

REYNALDO. You want me to smile?

TOM. I demand it.

REYNALDO. You what?

TOM. The tourist is always right.

REYNALDO. What?

TOM. Isn't that your country's motto?

REYNALDO. Not mine.

TOM. Didn't it take over for "country or death, we will be victorious?"

REYNALDO. Not in my book.

TOM. It has in mine.

REYNALDO. I see.

TOM. Good. I'm glad. Smile!

REYNALDO. Alright. Here is a smile.

(**REYNALDO** *smiles angrily at* **TOM.**)

TOM. Angry.

REYNALDO. Yes.

TOM. Angry revolutionary.

REYNALDO. Right.

TOM. That's not what your country sells anymore.

REYNALDO. I don't think you're right.

TOM. You know I am right.

REYNALDO. Well...

TOM. Don't you?

REYNALDO. Unfortunately, it seems, we are in the middle of a special period in our development...

TOM. I'm right. Admit it.

REYNALDO. Yes.

TOM. That wasn't hard, was it?

REYNALDO. Actually, it was.

TOM. You are a tourist economy.

REYNALDO. Because of the fall of the U.S.S.R...

TOM. I know.

REYNALDO. It's become impossible.

TOM. You want to change all that. I know you do!

REYNALDO. Is this a better smile?

(**REYNALDO** *smiles a sexy smile.*)

TOM. Seductive.

REYNALDO. Take your picture.

(**TOM** *takes a picture.*)

TOM. I like taking pictures of the exotic.

REYNALDO. You think I am exotic?

TOM. Not just you, all of you.

REYNALDO. Really?

TOM. All of you Cubans are exotica.

REYNALDO. I thought we were a threat.

TOM. Everything exotic is a threat in the good old U.S.A.

REYNALDO. No more pictures.

TOM. Hot Latins. Tempting to us Gringos. Why else would
    Papa Hemingway have come here so often?

REYNALDO. For our fishing.

TOM. I don't think so.

(**TOM** *takes a picture.*)

REYNALDO. For our weather.

TOM. God, I wish you were wearing short shorts.

REYNALDO. What?

TOM. Blue jeans that are cut off.

REYNALDO. What is your...

TOM. My what? Fucking problem.

REYNALDO. Yes.

TOM. What is my fucking problem?

REYNALDO. That's right.

TOM. That I want to look like I am a faggot tourist out for a wild day in La Habana.

REYNALDO. I see.

TOM. And that I am just trying to pick up some twenty-dollar whore like you.

REYNALDO. I'm too old to be a whore.

TOM. It takes all kinds.

REYNALDO. True.

TOM. I have a Daddy fixation.

REYNALDO. Do you?

TOM. Like you Cubans and Fidel.

REYNALDO. Stop it.

TOM. Have I gone too far?

REYNALDO. I don't think Fidel is my father.

TOM. Grandfather?

REYNALDO. Fidel is no family of mine.

TOM. Come on, show some skin.

REYNALDO. Stop this.

TOM. Forget it.

REYNALDO. Fine.

TOM. You look too much like an intellectual to be anyone I'd be interested in. Do you have some cigars that you can offer to sell me?

REYNALDO. No.

TOM. Great. Do you have a girlfriend waiting in a car that can come over and kiss my neck?

REYNALDO. Absolutely not.

TOM. Then what the fuck is an American doing here talking to you?

REYNALDO. To find out the history of this place?

TOM. I'm an American, we do not give a flying fuck about history. Come on.

REYNALDO. True.

TOM. Only fucking faggots come here to get laid. Or old men with beer bellies, and the only way they can get a young girl is a communist country.

REYNALDO. I thought it was because we were intoxicating.

TOM. Who told you that?

REYNALDO. Gringos. Gringos like you.

TOM. We are going to be noticed.

REYNALDO. Don't worry. I will take off my shirt and let you take a picture.

(**REYNALDO** *takes off his shirt and smiles.* **TOM** *takes a picture or two.*)

TOM. Nice chest.

REYNALDO. Thank you.

TOM. Played lots of sports, I bet.

REYNALDO. As a kid.

TOM. Baseball.

REYNALDO. No.

(**TOM** *takes a picture.*)

TOM. What kind?

REYNALDO. What?

TOM. What kind of sports team were you on?

REYNALDO. Soccer.

TOM. Soccer, a lot of running and kicking.

REYNALDO. Yes.

TOM. Running and kicking, good thing if you live in a third world country.

REYNALDO. Oh, come on.

(**TOM** *takes a picture.*)

REYNALDO. How many more pictures?

TOM. So I bet you have nice legs, also.

REYNALDO. I am not going to take off my pants.

TOM. Fine. This is enough.

REYNALDO. Why don't you buy me a beer?

TOM. Thirsty?

REYNALDO. Cuban security knows that a Cuban man will do anything for a beer.

TOM. Good one.

REYNALDO. Trying to play my part.

TOM. Of whore?

REYNALDO. Yes.

TOM. Where should I get the beer?

REYNALDO. Across the street.

TOM. Why don't I send you to buy it?

REYNALDO. Didn't your mother teach you any manners?

TOM. What?

REYNALDO. I'm a whore, not an errand boy.

TOM. Right.

REYNALDO. I know I'm right. So?

TOM. What?

REYNALDO. Get it!

TOM. Be right back.

(**TOM** *leaves.*)

REYNALDO. Fuck! Maybe it is too soon. Maybe I should leave. No, fuck. Fuck it! Now. Now. The moment is now. What fucking bastards Gringos are. They have destroyed most of the world. For profit. Not even an ideology – well, not true. Profit is their ideology. But they can help me.

(**TOM** *comes back, gives* **REYNALDO** *the beer.*)

REYNALDO. Thank you.

TOM. I thought the Nacional was too obvious.

REYNALDO. Who knows?

TOM. You can button your shirt now.

REYNALDO. Right.

TOM. I mean. I'm not a fag.

REYNALDO. Sure.

(**REYNALDO** *buttons his shirt.*)

TOM. I mean, that's my cover. Fag tourist from San Francisco...that's only 'cause I hear the female whores are informants.

REYNALDO. I don't know anything about that.

TOM. I know you're a good guy.

REYNALDO. I try.

TOM. I am here to help you.

REYNALDO. We appreciate it. Who sent you?

TOM. That's not important.

REYNALDO. It is to me. George W. Bush?

TOM. Let's just say people who are interested in Cuba.

REYNALDO. Church group? Jeb Bush?

TOM. People interested in Cuba. That's all I can say.

REYNALDO. Are you CIA?

TOM. Do you really think I'd answer that?

REYNALDO. I'm sure you will when I fuck you with my big Cuban cock.

TOM. Watch it, fellow! You don't know who you are fucking with!

REYNALDO. Precisely. I want to know who you are.

TOM. Business man who is interested in cleaning up Cuba.

REYNALDO. Cubans can clean up Cuba.

TOM. But we are interested in helping you clean it up.

REYNALDO. At what price?

TOM. Communication...

REYNALDO. Of what kind?

TOM. To help you rejoin the human race.

REYNALDO. I've been to other countries in Latin America. Believe me, I don't want my country to turn into that.

TOM. I said the human race.

REYNALDO. What?

TOM. You've never been to the U.S.A. You don't know what that life is like.

REYNALDO. I have been there, you fucking prick. Forget it.

(**REYNALDO** *starts to walk away.*)

TOM. Come on.

REYNALDO. Forget it!

TOM. I'm sorry. I'm arrogant.

REYNALDO. You are.

TOM. Bad habit.

REYNALDO. Trait.

TOM. What?

REYNALDO. Capitalist arrogance, an American trait.

TOM. And you don't want to have it?

REYNALDO. What?

TOM. To be an arrogant American?

REYNALDO. You have no idea who I am.

TOM. Let's communicate.

REYNALDO. How?

TOM. We want to help you.

REYNALDO. Help me how?

TOM. To bring democracy to this fallen Paradise.

REYNALDO. You are C.I.A.

TOM. Come on.

REYNALDO. How can I trust you?

TOM. I'm a religious man who believes in democracy.

REYNALDO. Baptist?

TOM. Yes.

REYNALDO. You don't work for the government?

TOM. No.

REYNALDO. Now I have two choices.

TOM. Really. What are they?

REYNALDO. To believe you, even though I know you are lying.

TOM. That's one.

REYNALDO. Or walk away.

(*They look at each other.*)

TOM. One of your eyes is lighter than the other.

REYNALDO. You notice everything.

TOM. Yes, I do.

REYNALDO. Your eyes are bloodshot.

TOM. Too much seven year-old rum.

REYNALDO. Are you a man of God?

TOM. Yes, I am.

REYNALDO. I see.

TOM. So I guess it's choice number one.

REYNALDO. What?

TOM. You haven't walked away.

REYNALDO. That's true.

TOM. We know you have a library. We know you are an artist. We want to get you a computer. We will create you a web site so you can play your music to the world.

REYNALDO. They control the web. It's hard to get access.

TOM. We will get it for you.

REYNALDO. How?

TOM. We have friends in the system.

REYNALDO. Who?

TOM. Baptists.

REYNALDO. I guess you are everywhere.

TOM. Doesn't that make you happy?

REYNALDO. I don't know.

TOM. We want to give you books. We can directly feed you information. We can make your library the center of information for the island. We can help you change this country from the inside. And we will stay out of it.

REYNALDO. You're not Baptist.

TOM. No. But you are a dissident.

REYNALDO. Yes.

TOM. So let us help you.

REYNALDO. I need to see my brother.

TOM. He's dying, yes?

REYNALDO. Yes, I will come back and forth. Artists can do that, right?

TOM. Others have.

REYNALDO. Cuba has to be sovereign. Change from within.

TOM. We want that.

REYNALDO. I have to go.

TOM. Take this.

REYNALDO. What?

TOM. A book.

(REYNALDO *takes the book.*)

REYNALDO. *Moby Dick.*

TOM. An American classic.

REYNALDO. Yes.

TOM. About searching for the unattainable on the high seas.

REYNALDO. Like this island.

TOM. Yes, and we will find it.

REYNALDO. And kill the Revolution.

TOM. Turn it into something else.

REYNALDO. Fuel for capitalism.

TOM. A jewel in the crown.

REYNALDO. I don't want the book.

TOM. There's twenty thousand dollars inside. We know you need it for your art, we want your help. Twenty thousand was all we could get into the book.

REYNALDO. Maybe you should have given me *War and Peace.*

TOM. That is a Russian book.

REYNALDO. But Tolstoy was not a Communist!

(TOM *walks away.*)

REYNALDO. Should I follow you? Should I throw the book into the ocean? Or should I take the money.

(*He thinks about it. We hear Cuban rap.*)

REYNALDO. Rap. Jesus!

(He sits on El Malecon and begins to read. He flips though the pages.)

REYNALDO. There's money on every page, fifties and hundreds. How the hell am I going to change hundreds?

(Blackout.)

Scene Four

(Slide: The Nacional Hotel. The bar. Later that night.)

*(***RUTH*** sits alone. She is drinking a mojito. She talks into her tape recorder.)*

RUTH. Here I have begun to forget my troubles waiting for me back there in the ivory towers of the sacred Ivy League. With him...I won't mention his name. It is so sensual and free here...Yet dialectical...they seem to have a complete view of the world, a view Americans do not as a whole have...maybe that's why I was so drawn...to the Eastern block...to him...To my...don't mention his name...I am talking to you from a bar at The Nacional Hotel...it's empty...Summer is not tourist season...But I like it empty. It's full of ghosts. Out the window you can see a very large pool...surrounded by Greek-like statues...all beautiful, all tasteful...As if the people who once lived here were trying to create... Well not trying...did create Paris in the middle of the Caribbean sea...and then they made it Moscow... Moscow without the snow. Inside, the walls are lined with pictures of Che and Fidel mixed with nineteen-thirties movie stars. Fred Astaire, Errol Flynn, some from the forties, Ava Gardner looking tempting. What did she find in Havana? Oh, and Mariel Hemingway and Geraldine Chaplin, and my God, even Jill Clayburgh...I remember her in *An Unmarried Woman...* she reminded me of myself. And there's Cantinflas, the Mexican clown...They have a film festival here every December, that's when the celebs come...the bar is filled with the ghosts of cigarettes and gangsters.

More like Hollywood than Hollywood has ever been...
To be in love here must be a wonderful thing...the sea
hits the walls of El Malecon...the wind caresses your
hair, you can feel it touch the inside of your thighs
and I think of you. Oh, God, I am in paradise and still
thinking of you, my darling...No! You must not say his
name! I met a man. He's a conductor. I am going to
his house for dinner...So easy. They make it so easy for
a stranger...

(**TOM** *walks in. He looks drunk.*)

RUTH. A man has just walked in. Maybe I should stop
recording. He might be an American...no, I bet he's
German or Swiss...Danish maybe.

TOM. Howdy, stranger.

RUTH. Oh God, no. American....

TOM. Are you talking to yourself?

RUTH. No, I'm recording...

TOM. What?

RUTH. My thoughts, my journal.

TOM. Journal...

RUTH. Yes.

TOM. Of your vacation?

RUTH. Sure.

TOM. Your Havana Journal?

RUTH. You could say that.

TOM. Well...my Havana Journal is full of pain...

RUTH. Really?

TOM. Do you mind turning that tape recorder off?

RUTH. I'm sorry.

TOM. You never know who is an informant in this country,
believe you me!

RUTH. For which side?

TOM. Both.

RUTH. I'll turn it off.

(RUTH turns off the tape recorder.)

TOM. Good. Now...my Havana Journal is sad because I have fallen in love.

RUTH. On this trip?

TOM. This trip? Are you kidding, this is my sixth trip here in the last three months, and I am so afraid that I'm going to get caught and fined fifty-thousand dollars by our government...

RUTH. What?

TOM. That's how much they fine you. If they find out...The Treasury Department...that you have been spending dollars here.

RUTH. I see. Right. But they don't ever really do that, do they?

TOM. There was this woman in her seventies who wrote a book about biking in Cuba, and they fined her.

RUTH. Did she fight it?

TOM. Yes.

RUTH. Did she pay the fine?

TOM. I don't know.

RUTH. Is it worth it?

TOM. What?

RUTH. To do something illegal for love.

TOM. No matter how you look at it, there's a price.

RUTH. In love?

TOM. Believe me, I have been spending dollars here because I'm smitten. Can you tell how smitten I am?

RUTH. Who's the lucky Señorita?

TOM. Señor.

RUTH. Oh, I see.

TOM. Actually, more like Señorito. He's only eighteen.

RUTH. You rascal.

TOM. You're not judging me?

RUTH. I don't believe in standard sexual morality.

TOM. Were you a hippie in the sixties?

RUTH. I was a radical.

TOM. Really?

RUTH. Yes.

TOM. Against the Vietnam War and all that?

RUTH. Absolutely.

TOM. Another Hanoi Jane?

RUTH. Hardly. I was to the left of Jane Fonda.

TOM. Right. Want to see his picture?

RUTH. Sure.

(**TOM** *takes out a picture from his wallet.*)

TOM. Isn't he beautiful? God.

RUTH. Well, he is young.

TOM. He could be a model, don't you think?

RUTH. If that's something you care about.

TOM. In the States, a guy like this, who looks like this, would never give me the time of day.

RUTH. Young people are like that.

TOM. You don't know how vicious queens can be.

RUTH. You should meet some of my students. Viciousness I know.

TOM. Talk about being invisible after you turn a certain age...

RUTH. That's not something that ever happens to a man.

TOM. If you're a gay guy and old, it's worse than being a woman and old.

RUTH. How about guys your own age?

TOM. Most guys my age died.

RUTH. Sorry. Right.

TOM. The ones I loved anyway.

RUTH. Sometimes I forget about that.

TOM. A lot of people made it through...

RUTH. Like you.

TOM. What?

RUTH. You survived.

TOM. Yes, I did. And God brought me this angel. I would do anything for him. I do anything for him, I bought him a house here. I support his whole family. But now things are getting tough for him in his home town...

RUTH. Are you sure? I mean, that he loves you. He has told you that he loves you. Right?

TOM. He has shown it to me.

RUTH. You are sure about this? I would hate seeing a nice guy like you get hurt.

TOM. Listen, his family, his town, has turned against him because of our love. They might be revolutionaries. But believe me, they are homophobic. Bastards. My poor baby.

RUTH. Maybe he can try to win that lottery. Where you get to leave...legally. Maybe you should tell him to sign up for it?

TOM. It would not be good for him. If people heard he signed up for the lottery. This country is very unforgiving of people that want to leave it. He doesn't live in Havana, he lives in another province, Pinar del Rio, and believe me things in Pinar Del Rio are a lot different than they are in Havana. It's like the difference between San Francisco and Dallas...when it comes to the gay thing. Look at him. I can look at him. He is, Jesus, the hottest man I have ever known. I've got to put it away. I get horny just from the picture...

(**TOM** *puts the picture back in his wallet.*)

The hottest man I have ever known. A sex god. And the thing is, he really loves me. You believe me, don't you?

RUTH. I just hope you don't get hurt.

TOM. His name is Julio, my Juliet. I die when I am in Gainesville all by myself, with him less than two hundred miles away, but an iron fence the height of the twin towers is keeping us apart...You know what I mean?

RUTH. I know all about the Embargo.

TOM. No. Not the Embargo. Fuck the Embargo! Love! Obsessive love.

RUTH. I have a Ph.D. in obsessive love.

TOM. Really?

RUTH. Yes, a sixty-five year-old Czech short story writer who thinks I am too old for him.

TOM. You like the foreign meat?

RUTH. Yes, I do.

TOM. So do I.

RUTH. Here's to us!

(They toast.)

TOM. How am I going to get him to America? He got beat up in his hometown for loving me. He's been getting threats. We try to play it straight, but I am afraid I stand out.

RUTH. I'm sure you do.

TOM. I gotta get him out of his town.

RUTH. Bring him to Havana.

TOM. You think that's easy? You can't move to Havana without a permit. Havana is overcrowded, you need a special permit to live here. You are not free in this country to move like we are in America...

RUTH. I didn't know that.

TOM. This is not the paradise you think it is.

RUTH. I don't know about that...

TOM. Do you know anyone that is taking people illegally across the waters?

RUTH. What are you talking about?

TOM. I have to get him on a boat out of here. I am willing to pay. I just need names of people doing the job.

RUTH. I don't know anyone.

TOM. Are you sure?

RUTH. I don't know anyone here.

TOM. I don't believe you.

RUTH. I'm a tourist.

TOM. I didn't know radicals went on vacation.

RUTH. We do.

TOM. I'm sorry. I'm just desperate.

RUTH. I see that.

TOM. How will I ever get my honey out?

RUTH. Vote against George W. Bush.

TOM. Leave politics out of all this.

RUTH. What are you talking about? This is all about politics, the reason why there is an Embargo towards Cuba is because of a right wing agenda...About control of the world...

TOM. Why should we not control the world?

RUTH. What are you saying?

TOM. Somebody has to. Why not us?

RUTH. Because we don't have the right to manifest destiny. If you want the Embargo to end, get the right-wingers out of office. Believe me, it's your last chance to get your baby out of here.

TOM. I'm not a Democrat, and I'm not a liberal. I believe in the right's plans for America.

RUTH. What?

TOM. I'm a log cabin Republican.

RUTH. You mean a self-hating fag.

TOM. Hey, watch it you liberal whore!

RUTH. Fuck you.

TOM. Love your country, or fucking leave it.

RUTH. You know what, we are in a Marxist country. Fuck you and your politics. I hope Julio is scamming you. He doesn't love you, you know.

TOM. How do you know?

RUTH. 'Cause you are not good enough for him. You are right. I hope he is taking you for every penny you have 'cause that's what you deserve. You want to rape this country.

TOM. How about you?

RUTH. I believe in their ideals.

TOM. Ideals? They are third world.

RUTH. Leave my table.

TOM. Listen to logic...

RUTH. Just go.

TOM. Listen, the great thing about America is that we can disagree.

RUTH. The great thing about my world, is that I don't have to listen to people like you. So go away.

TOM. That's not very nice.

RUTH. Neither is the war in Iraq.

TOM. Keep Iraq out of this.

RUTH. Fine, now goodbye.

TOM. Let me buy you a drink.

RUTH. I don't want anything from somebody like you. Do you get it? Get the fuck away from my table 'cause I will call security. Okay?

TOM. You have contempt for me, don't you?

RUTH. Yes, I do.

TOM. I'm your brother.

RUTH. You are no brother of mine.

TOM. Countryman then?

RUTH. Florida and New York are two different countries. Good night.

(She gets up to leave.)

TOM. You going?

RUTH. I came to Cuba to get away from people like you.

TOM. Let me buy you a drink?

RUTH. I don't drink with the likes of you.

TOM. Are you going to call security?

RUTH. I'm just going to find another bar.

TOM. Why?

RUTH. 'Cause I don't want to waste one more Goddamn second on people like you. Get it?

(**RUTH** *goes.*)

TOM. You don't know what we have planned for you. You liberal, leftist, cocksucking whore.

(*He screams.*)

Hey, bartender. Niño! Boy! I need a fucking drink!

(*Blackout.*)

Scene Five

(*Slide: Miami Airport, a week later. In front of La Carreta Cuban coffee stand.*)

(**RUTH** *and* **REYNALDO** *are drinking cafes.*)

RUTH. I didn't hear from you about dinner...imagine my surprise when I saw you on the plane.

REYNALDO. I will make you the roast pork here.

RUTH. How about the all women classical orchestra?

REYNALDO. They will go on without me.

RUTH. So much for your passion.

REYNALDO. Yes.

RUTH. Did you pay for it with Janet's money?

REYNALDO. What?

RUTH. Your exodus from your country?

REYNALDO. No. That's not nearly enough money for an exit visa.

RUTH. Then how?

REYNALDO. I work for the C.I.A. I shouldn't be telling you this. I will be coming in and out of Cuba more easily... it will help my classical music career.

RUTH. How about socialism?

REYNALDO. Socialism is dead.

RUTH. No it's not, it never will be dead.

REYNALDO. You shouldn't talk like that.

RUTH. Like what?

REYNALDO. So openly.

RUTH. This is America.

REYNALDO. Exactly.

RUTH. You're betraying everything you believe in.

REYNALDO. For the good of my art.

RUTH. You'll never have an orchestra here.

REYNALDO. I am going to arrange for Gloria Estefan and her husband. That's why I am officially here. One of the few cultural exchanges, there won't be any press. They don't like that I am going back and forth.

RUTH. Who?

REYNALDO. Gloria.

RUTH. They are popular music!

REYNALDO. One must go with the times we live in.

RUTH. Your country gave you everything.

REYNALDO. I needed more.

RUTH. What?

REYNALDO. A house with a pool like my brother.

RUTH. Capitalism is the death of art.

REYNALDO. They have you bugged. I would be careful what you say.

RUTH. Who had me bugged?

REYNALDO. George W.

RUTH. You have proof?

REYNALDO. I am telling you this because I like you.

RUTH. Like me?

REYNALDO. Yes.

RUTH. I don't respect you anymore.

REYNALDO. Good-bye.

RUTH. Yes.

REYNALDO. Be careful.

RUTH. You are not ever going back to your orchestra.

REYNALDO. The cafe here is better than in Cuba.

(*He walks away.*)

RUTH. Am I the last standing Marxist?

(She takes out her tape recorder.)

RUTH. Are you bugged? Are you listening to me?

(Blackout.)

(The men sing.)

MEN.
TAKE A CUP OF HOLY WATER
THEN PERFUME THE SWEET WARM WATER.
FILL YOUR SOUL TO OVERFLOWING
FOR OUR JOURNEY WITH YEMAYA.
YEMAYA, YEMAYA.

TASTE THE SALT WITHIN YOUR TEARS
NEVER SEEK TO HIDE THEM
TELL HER ALL YOUR DREAMS AND FEARS
AND THE QUEEN WILL GUIDE THEM
SWEET YEMAYA
SWEET YEMAYA
SWEET YEMAYA

WE HAVE PLACED
OUR CUP OF WATER,
WE HAVE FILLED A JAR WITH HONEY.
AND WE DRINK THE CANE'S SWEET NECTAR
AND YOUR BOWL IS FILLED WITH SEA.
COME AND JOIN OUR SACRED PARTY.
FILL OUR SOULS TO OVERFLOWING
DO NOT HIDE
BE OUR GUIDE
HELP US FIND YOUR TRUEST MEANING.
SWEET YEMAYA
SWEET YEMAYA
SWEET YEMAYA
SWEET YEMAYA

REYNALDO. Sweet Yemaya…
Sweet Yemaya…

Scene Six

(Slide: Columbia University, November 1, 2004.)

(Columbia University. Ruth's office. Late at night. **RUTH** *has opened a bottle of vodka. She pours it into a coffee cup. She is talking to the tape.)*

RUTH. Janeane said that tomorrow is just the beginning. Maybe...But really, Janeane, do you think there is room for me on Air America? My voice is too radical, even for you. Oh God, why wasn't I born a European? Or Slavic? Or a Latin American? Or a Cuban reading my Marx everyday...Why was I not born in Cuba? I would never run from a third world country...not like the son of a bitch, Reynaldo....Sandor...forget him. Slam the door on that one, Ruth. We are a day away. One day away from the election. Two or three days ago we had a partial eclipse of the moon, then Halloween last night it was windy and warm...and today it is windy and cold. Today is All Saints' Day...Tomorrow, the Day of the Dead....Here I am at Columbia, New York. In this vault of middlebrow intellectualism...On All Saints' Day, November 1, 2004. Tomorrow is Election Day in the good old USA....Everyone is afraid that their vote will not be counted! It is the beginning of the end of the Yankee empire...Remember the Maine, as the Cubans would say...Remember Vietnam, Nicaragua...Iraq... Oh, God...so many names to remember...such a long list...In the Sudan right now the Sudanese military has just surrounded all the refugee camps, and they could be slaughtering them right now. At this moment. Women are being raped. I will go vote. I will go vote. I will go vote! Although I know that my voice will not be counted, not by the left, not by the right. My voice could only be heard if I began to scream at the top of my lungs. Blood, murderers. You murder women like me. Women with a mind! And a fucking point of view, an artistic political voice...this country has no use for us. Sandor has no use for me! Sandor found a young protégée in the south of France. But I do not hate her for it. I hate Sandor and his power at sixty-five because he is a fucking man. He won't speak to me anymore. The little protégée does not like it. Fucking men!! Fuck you, Sandor. God, Sandor? Sandor?

(A knock on the door.)

RUTH. Sandor?

IVAN. No, Ivan.

RUTH. Ivan?

IVAN. Any trash?

RUTH. Yes, come in.

(IVAN comes in.)

RUTH. Are you ever going to vacuum?

IVAN. Tonight, if you like?

RUTH. No, not tonight.

IVAN. Why not?

RUTH. Tonight I don't understand anything.

IVAN. About?

RUTH. About myself.

IVAN. We are all a mystery.

RUTH. About the world.

IVAN. The world?

RUTH. Yes!

(IVAN picks up a key.)

IVAN. The key to your filing cabinet.

RUTH. What?

IVAN. It was on the floor.

RUTH. How do you know it went to my filing cabinet?

IVAN. Lucky guess.

RUTH. Did you hear me just now?

IVAN. No.

RUTH. Are you sure?

IVAN. I would not have disturbed you.

RUTH. You've heard me before?

IVAN. Yes, I'm afraid that I have.

RUTH. And Sandor?

IVAN. Excuse me.

RUTH. Don't be shy.

IVAN. I just clean the trash. Right?

RUTH. You've answered me.

IVAN. Sometimes there are more answers in silence than in words.

RUTH. You did grow up under communism.

IVAN. Why do you say that?

RUTH. The double talk.

IVAN. One has to be careful. When one is a foreigner.

RUTH. I can imagine.

IVAN. Good.

RUTH. Especially a foreigner from a former communist country.

IVAN. My country? Yes, we were "Red."

RUTH. With a capital R.

IVAN. Yes.

RUTH. So am I.

IVAN. Not anarchist?

RUTH. Both.

IVAN. An anarchist and a communist?

RUTH. That's right.

IVAN. That's like a time bomb.

RUTH. Sometimes I feel like I will explode.

IVAN. I know the feeling.

RUTH. I have gotten a grant to write about third world countries. I have started with one near by. Cuba.

IVAN. They lived under Russia's thumb.

RUTH. They're still Communist.

IVAN. Yes.

RUTH. And Russia is gone.

IVAN. The former Soviet Union is gone.

RUTH. Right.

IVAN. Communism is gone.

RUTH. True.

IVAN. Russia is still there. With its iron fist, believe me!

RUTH. Capitalist now.

IVAN. And mobsters.

RUTH. Of course.

IVAN. Terrible. Communism is terrible!

RUTH. In some places.

IVAN. Everywhere.

RUTH. Cuba seemed very idealistic.

IVAN. From far away everything looks pretty.

RUTH. We have an embargo against them. It's illegal for me to go.

IVAN. But you went.

RUTH. I am willing to get arrested.

IVAN. For what you believe in?

RUTH. That's right.

IVAN. You like danger.

RUTH. I do.

IVAN. I should vacuum your rug.

(IVAN *goes out the door.*)

RUTH. What?

(IVAN *walks back in with a vacuum cleaner and turns it on.* RUTH *takes a swig from the vodka bottle. She looks lost.*)

How the hell am I going to finish all of this?

(*Her phone rings.*)

Who the hell would call me? A student? (*She picks up the phone.*) No, no meeting tonight. I am going home!

(RUTH *hangs up the phone.*)

IVAN. Student?

RUTH. Vampire!

IVAN. Vampire?

RUTH. Students are all vampires.

IVAN. They want your blood?

RUTH. Everything.

IVAN. Spoiled.

RUTH. Yes, very.

IVAN. I work.

RUTH. So do I.

IVAN. With my hands and my back.

RUTH. Working with your mind is harder.

IVAN. Sure. If that's what you want to believe.

RUTH. I better read this.

(**RUTH** *picks up a manuscript. Ruth tries to read.*)

RUTH. Let go for God's fucking sake.

IVAN. I go.

RUTH. No, I was talking to the manuscript.

IVAN. Your students?

RUTH. Listen to this: "I walked out of the elevator. Every woman in the room looked at me. I have become, I have begun, I thought to myself. I am good looking..." Blah, blah, blah.....

IVAN. Good looking?

RUTH. Shit, I lost my place. Can't find it. Want a sip?

(**RUTH** *looks up.*)

IVAN. No, thank you.

RUTH. I feel so sorry for the human race.

IVAN. So do I.

RUTH. I feel sorry for all of them.

IVAN. For who?

RUTH. The Native Americans, the blacks, the Turks, the Greeks, the Armenians, the Jews, the Palestinians, the Nicaraguans, the Vietnamese, the Cambodians... Rwanda, Bosnia, Chile...all the Martyrs that have died in vain.

IVAN. I'm sure, but you are perceived as evil.

RUTH. Who?

IVAN. Americans. I'm sorry. Should not have said that.

RUTH. But we are.

IVAN. You agree?

RUTH. Yes.

IVAN. Very good.

RUTH. Thank you.

IVAN. Yes, well...I should...

RUTH. Are you done?

IVAN. No, I am not.

RUTH. Then you should vacuum and I should read.

IVAN. Of course.

RUTH. I have a lot of work to finish.

IVAN. I must vacuum.

RUTH. Go ahead.

(**IVAN** *vacuums.* **RUTH** *works.*)

IVAN. Good night.

(**IVAN** *leaves.* **RUTH** *looks at the manuscript.*)

RUTH. Nothing but dried leaves. Passionless. I will find... Something. Something, please!

(**RUTH** *reads. We hear a door close.*)

Sandor, could you not stay away from my mind? Sandor?

(**IVAN** *opens the door. He walks in.*)

IVAN. Sorry to disappoint you.

RUTH. The Russian, not the Czech.

IVAN. Former Soviet Union.

RUTH. Right.

IVAN. Not Russia.

RUTH. Yes.

IVAN. Good, we got that straight.

RUTH. Yes.

IVAN. Definitions are important.

RUTH. Of course.

IVAN. I know you understand that.

    (**RUTH** *looks through some papers.* **IVAN** *stands in front of her.*)

RUTH. Don't you have something to do?

IVAN. Clean your office.

RUTH. You vacuumed. What else?

IVAN. I see.

RUTH. What do you mean by that?

IVAN. Not even Cuba taught you how to treat the proletariat.

RUTH. What?

IVAN. How was Havana?

RUTH. Revolutionary.

IVAN. Really?

RUTH. A bolt of lighting. A spark of genius.

IVAN. Fidel?

RUTH. The country. The people. Real struggle.

IVAN. All struggle is real.

RUTH. What?

IVAN. Everybody has got to survive.

RUTH. Well, you see...ah...oh, my God...I've forgotten your name.

IVAN. Ivan.

RUTH. Yes, Ivan. Right. Of course. I'm...

IVAN. Ruth. I know.

RUTH. You remembered mine?

IVAN. I stayed.

RUTH. What?

IVAN. Here all summer at Columbia. No escape for me.

RUTH. Yes, of course.

IVAN. Same floors, same drinking fountains, same toilets to clean.

RUTH. I'm so sorry.

IVAN. This place...

RUTH. Columbia?

IVAN. No, this office.

RUTH. Yes?

IVAN. This office is haunted by you.

RUTH. Is it?

IVAN. Your presence is always here. Ruth...Ruth...in the walls...

RUTH. I don't believe you.

IVAN. It's the truth.

RUTH. The truth?

IVAN. I feel you everywhere.

RUTH. You feel me?

IVAN. I do.

RUTH. That's very flattering. Thank you.

IVAN. Sure.

RUTH. Well...

IVAN. Ruth everywhere...in the air.

RUTH. It's just 'cause I am always here late at night.

IVAN. Yes, you are.

RUTH. The two of us.

IVAN. And sometimes Sandor.

RUTH. Right.

IVAN. But he's been away lately.

RUTH. He's in training.

IVAN. For what?

RUTH. His second childhood.

IVAN. What?

RUTH. Never mind.

IVAN. You don't like him anymore.

RUTH. No, I don't.

IVAN. I think that's better.

(RUTH *does not know what to say.*)

RUTH. Well...

IVAN. Better for you.

RUTH. I've been back for two months, longer. I hadn't seen you. Or heard you until tonight.

IVAN. I'm very quiet and secretive. But tonight I decided to talk to you.

RUTH That's why you came and vacuumed?

IVAN. My way of survival.

RUTH. Really?

IVAN. Yes.

RUTH. I see.

IVAN. I was taught if you keep quiet, they won't notice you.

RUTH. I wish I knew that trick.

IVAN. Back home. They teach you that trick from birth.

RUTH. Where are you from?

IVAN. The former Soviet Union.

RUTH. No, what part...

IVAN. Guess...

RUTH. Moscow?

IVAN. Never.

RUTH. Leningrad...I mean Saint Petersburg.

IVAN. I told you, not Russia.

RUTH. The Ukraine?

IVAN. Impossible.

RUTH. Where then? Tell me!

IVAN. Chechnya.

RUTH. Not a very popular place right now.

IVAN. I know....

RUTH. Brutal countrymen you have.

IVAN. I know.

RUTH. Good.

IVAN. So do you.

RUTH. What?

IVAN. Your countrymen are brutal.

RUTH. I realize that but...

IVAN. I know. I know. Terrorists are not very popular.

RUTH. I suppose not.

IVAN. In communism. You learn how be quiet.

RUTH. Really?

IVAN. Anyone can be listening to your thoughts.

RUTH. I see.

IVAN. Do you?

\RUTH. Yes, I have been to Cuba after all.

IVAN. And in Cuba you learned to forget your troubles here. They became insignificant... Cuba was so sensual, yet dialectical...

RUTH. What?

IVAN. Cuba was so sensual and free.

RUTH. If I didn't know better, I'd think you were quoting me.

IVAN. I picked up your trash. Now I go.

(*IVAN starts to go.*)

RUTH. You've listened to my tapes.

(*IVAN starts to empty the trash.*)

Haven't you?

(*He keeps cleaning.*)

Stop cleaning and answer me.

(*He sits.*)

IVAN. Yes.

RUTH. You have to go.

IVAN. All summer.

RUTH. Oh, my God!

IVAN. And most of this fall...

RUTH. How dare you! That's my journal, private...

IVAN. Why do you make them?

RUTH. None of your business.

IVAN. I want to know.

RUTH. Why?

IVAN. I have to know. Please.

RUTH. My mother had Alzheimer's. In the end she had forgotten everything.

IVAN. Everything?

RUTH. Including me.

IVAN. I'm sorry.

RUTH. And I want to remember who I was.

IVAN. A radical?

RUTH. Yes, what I represented in the times when I lived.

IVAN. You should find a better hiding place for the key. Your assistant could find it easily. Or Sandor, or your students.

RUTH. I could have you fired.

IVAN. For what?

RUTH. Snooping.

IVAN. But you wanted someone to hear it.

RUTH. What?

IVAN. That's why you make them. To seduce Sandor. Instead you seduced another member of the Eastern block.

RUTH. Have I seduced you?

IVAN. Yes. With your willingness...

RUTH. To what?

IVAN. To be ugly.

RUTH. That's what I always tell my students, be willing to be ugly...

IVAN. These are ugly times. This country is turning into Russia. I see it, Russia under Stalin. It's like what I read in the history books, people being stupid, willing to give away the right to protest, to speak, to think... I think your tapes are dangerous. I think they should be played on the radio.

RUTH. Really?

IVAN. They are like an explosion.

RUTH. I'm so angry!

IVAN. I know.

RUTH. Oh, I don't think anyone knows how angry I really am!

IVAN. It does not scare me.

RUTH. You understand my anger?

IVAN. Yes, I do.

RUTH. I think you do.

IVAN. You can report me if you want.

RUTH. I won't have you fired.

IVAN. Good.

RUTH. You are beautiful.

IVAN. So are you.

RUTH. Well...You know so much about me and I know so little about you.

IVAN. I hide.

RUTH. Right.

IVAN. I don't want to be noticed.

RUTH. I see.

IVAN. But in the silences you can tell a story.

RUTH. Let me see.

(They look at each other for a long time. She hands him a drink. He takes it.)

IVAN. Thank you. Vodka.

RUTH. What an intimate moment we just had.

IVAN. Shh!

RUTH. Fine.

(He touches her hand. He goes to the tape recorder. He turns it on, he talks into it.)

IVAN. My brother and my sister died during a terrorist act. They committed the act. My country, my people, demand freedom from the tyrant. We will not remain quiet, we will be heard. All the silent ones, Ruth, we will be heard. In explosions, in gunfire...on a tape. My dear Ruth, we will be heard.

(She looks at him.)

RUTH. I'm beginning to understand.

IVAN. I knew you would.

(Blackout.)

End of play.

Also by
Eduardo Machado...

Broken Eggs

The Cook

Crocodile Eyes

Havana is Waiting

In the Eye of the Hurricane

Kissing Fidel

**The Modern Ladies
of Guanabacoa**

Once Removed

OTHER TITLES AVAILABLE FROM SAMUEL FRENCH

THE MODERN LADIES OF GUANABACOA

Eduardo Machado

Dark Comedy / 5m, 4f / Interior

The Modern Ladies of Guanabacoa shows one family's climb to wealth in the Cuba of 1928-31. The play is at once a political drama and social comedy, ranging from melodrama to farce. Questions of power, control and revolution within the family mirror society's wider conflicts. The father is a butcher who rules his wife and four grown children with an iron hand, even as he spends most of his time philandering outside the house. The only daughter, aged 27, is accused of having lost her virginity simply because she may once have kissed the now-deceased man who courted her for seven years. While her three brothers live less-cloistered sex lives, they benefit from a double standard that allows young Cuban men to go whoring to satisfy their "special needs."

"Mr. Machado uses both fast, clever dialogue and small farcical gags to capture the dislocations of this household on the brink of upheaval."
– *The New York Times*

www.ingramcontent.com/pod-product-compliance
Lightning Source LLC
Chambersburg PA
CBHW070417120726

47909CB00005B/1687